For Ruth

PUBLISHED BY DOUBLEDAY
a division of Bantam Doubleday Dell Publishing Group, Inc.
666 Fifth Avenue, New York, New York 10103

DOUBLEDAY
and the portrayal of an anchor with a dolphin
are trademarks of Doubleday,
a division of Bantam Doubleday Dell Publishing Group, Inc.

Library of Congress Cataloging-in-Publication Data
Brown, Ken (Ken James)
Why can't I fly?/Ken Brown.
p.   cm.
Summary: Ostrich fulfills a dream with a little help from his bird friends.
[1. Ostriches—Fiction.   2. Birds—Fiction.   3. Flight—Fiction.
4. Friendship—Fiction.] I. Title.
PZ7.B8157Wh   1990
[E]—dc20   89-39846 CIP AC
ISBN 0-385-41208-8
ISBN 0-385-41209-6 (lib. bdg.)

Copyright © 1990 by Ken Brown
First published by Andersen Press Ltd., 62-65 Chandos Place, London WC2.
Published in Australia by Century Hutchinson Australia Pty. Ltd., 89-91 Albion Street, Surry Hills, NSW 2010.

Why Can't I Fly?

Ken Brown

DOUBLEDAY

NEW YORK LONDON TORONTO SYDNEY AUCKLAND

Early one morning, all the animals were gathered, as usual, by the water.

"I wish I could fly," thought the Ostrich. "Why can't I fly?" he asked the Sparrow.

"Maybe your neck is too long," suggested the Sparrow.
"The flamingoes have long necks and they can fly,"
replied the Ostrich, "so why can't I?"

"I don't know," chirped the Sparrow, "perhaps your legs are too long."

"The storks have long legs and they can fly," said the Ostrich, "so why can't I?"

"Well, perhaps your wings are too small," said the Sparrow.

"You've got small wings and you can fly," answered the Ostrich, "so why can't I?"

"Well, I don't know! Maybe you just don't try hard enough," and so saying, the Sparrow flew away.

"Try hard enough indeed!"
thought the Ostrich. "I'll show him.

I'll show all of them that I can fly."

So he ran as fast as he could and,

flapping his wings, he
jumped off a high sand dune...

only to land, seconds later, with a terrible thud.

Next he climbed to the top of a huge rock.
"I'll show them!" he panted.
With his wings flailing the air, he threw himself over the edge, but instantly plunged downward and landed headfirst in the soft sand below.

He remained with his head in the sand, too embarrassed to show his face.

"I'll show them!" he thought. "If my wings are too small, I'll make them bigger."

Using some large leaves, bamboo canes, strong vines, and a great deal of skill, he constructed a flying machine.

Then he climbed to the top of the high rock again, and launched himself into the air.

"This is it! Look at me, everyone. I'm flying," cried the Ostrich.

But he spoke too soon! Moments later, he landed with an almighty splash right in the middle of the river.

"Never mind," said the Sparrow. "Your long neck will keep your head well above water!"

But the Ostrich was not put off by this, his first disastrous attempt at flying. He built another flying machine with even bigger wings and once again launched himself into the air.

"Out of my way!" he shouted to the doves. "Out of my way—I'm flying!"

Alas, this flight also ended in complete disaster, when
the Ostrich became totally entangled in the leaves of a
high palm tree.

"Never mind!" chirped the Sparrow. "Your long legs
will certainly help you to get down from there."

The Ostrich, however, was just as determined as ever to fly; he would not give up. So he built an even bigger flying machine and for the third time climbed to the top of the high rock. He took a deep breath and launched himself yet again into the air. This time, instead of plummeting straight downward as before, he soared high up into the sky, as gracefully as any other bird. "Look at me!" shouted the triumphant Ostrich. "Look, everybody, I'm flying!" But the only reply that he got was the sound of his own voice echoing about the empty skies.

The Ostrich couldn't understand it!

"Where is everyone?" he cried. "Where's Sparrow? I'm flying and there's no one here to see. They'll never believe me now."

But they did!